おばあちゃんの　サタデー　スープ

Grandma's Saturday Soup

Written by Sally Fraser

Illustrated by Derek Brazell

Japanese translation by Maiko & Noriko Osada

げつようびの　あさはやく　おかあさんに　おこされた。
「おきなさい、ミミ。さあ、きがえて　がっこうに　いくじかんよ。」
まだ　とっても　ねむかったけれど　わたしは　ベッドから
おきあがり　カーテンを　あけた。

Monday morning Mum woke me early.
"Get up Mimi and get dressed for school."
I climbed out of bed all sleepy and tired,
and pulled back the curtains.

くもっていて　さむそうな　あさだった。
そらに　うかぶ　くもは　しろくて
ふわふわしてた。
まるで　おばあちゃんが　どようびに
つくる　スープの　なかの　おだんごみたい。

The morning was cloudy and cold.

The clouds in the sky were white and fluffy.

They reminded me of the dumplings in Grandma's Saturday Soup.

おばあちゃんの　いえに　あそびに　いくと　おばあちゃんは
ジャマイカの　おはなしを　してくれる。

Grandma tells me stories about Jamaica when I go to her house.

「ジャマイカの　くもは　おおあめを　ふらせるの。
まるで　だれかが　おそらで　じゃぐちを
ひねったみたいに。あたたかい　かぜが　くもを
おいはらうと　また　おひさまが　かおを　だすのよ。」

"The clouds in Jamaica bring the heaviest rain.

It's like someone has turned the tap on in the sky.

The warm breeze moves them on and the sun comes out again."

かようびの　あさ　おとうさんが　がっこうへ　おくってくれた。
まえのよるに　ゆきが　ふったので　くうきは　つめたく
ひんやりと　していた。

Tuesday morning Dad took me to school.

The day was cold and crisp; it had snowed in the night.

ゆきに　さわると　すべすべしていて
きった　ヤマイモの　ひょうめんのよう。
まるで　おばあちゃんが　どようびに
つくる　スープに　はいっているような。

It's white and smooth and looked like the inside of a sliced yam.
Just like the yam in Grandma's Saturday Soup.

おばあちゃんは　ジャマイカの　かいがんの　しろい　すなは　つもりたての
ゆきみたいだけど　ぜんぜん　つめたくないんだって　おしえてくれた。

*Grandma tells me that the white powdery sand on the beaches looks
like fresh snow but it's never cold.*

しろい　すなで　すなダルマを　つくれるのかな？
できたら　おもしろいのに！

I wonder if I could make a sandman with the white sand?

Wouldn't that be funny?!

すいようびに　もっと　たくさん
ゆきが　ふった。さむかったけど
わたしは　たくさんの　ふくに
くるまって　あたたかくしてた。
おばあちゃんの　いえに　あそびに
いくと　いつも　ジャマイカの
おはなしを　してくれる。

Wednesday the snow fell harder. It was cold but I was wrapped up warm.

Grandma tells me stories about Jamaica when I go to her house.

「おひさまは　まいにち　かがやいているの。
おひさまは　とても　あたたかくて　はんずぼんと
はんそでの　シャツで　いいのよ。」
まいにち　あたたかい？　はんずぼんと　はんそでの
シャツ？　しんじられない。

"The sun shines every day. The sun is warm on your skin
and you only need to wear your shorts and a T-shirt."

Warm every day? Shorts and T-shirt? I can't believe that.

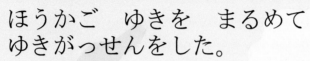

ほうかご　ゆきを　まるめて
ゆきがっせんをした。

At afternoon play we made snowballs
and threw them at each other.

The snowballs remind me of the round soft
potatoes in Grandma's Saturday Soup.

まるめた　ゆきは　まるで
おばあちゃんが　どようびに
つくる　スープの　なかの
じゃがいも　みたい。

もくようび　がっこうのあと　ともだちの
レイラと　レイラの　おかあさんと
としょかんに　いった。

On **Thursday** I went to the library
after school with my friend Layla
and her Mum.

こうえんの　そばを　とおったとき　きゅうこんの
めが　でてきているのに　きづいた。みどりの
めが　ゆきの　あいだから　のぞいている。
まるで　おばあちゃんが　どようびに　つくる
スープの　なかの　ねぎ　みたい。

As we passed the park we saw the little bulbs starting to grow.
The little green shoots poked through the snow. They looked like
the spring onions in Grandma's Saturday Soup.

Grandma tells me about the wonderful plants and flowers in Jamaica.
"In Jamaica the most beautiful flowers grow wild.
They are all different colours and sizes
and their smell fills the air."
I've never seen flowers like that before,
I wonder if she's only joking?

おばあちゃんは　ジャマイカの　すてきな
しょくぶつや　はなの　はなしを　してくれる。
「ジャマイカの　うつくしい　はなは　しぜんに
そだつの。いろも　おおきさも　みんな　ちがって、
その　かおりは　あたりいちめんに　ひろがるのよ。」
そんな　はなは　いちども　みたことが　ない。
おばあちゃんは　じょうだんを　いっているのかな？

きんようび おかあさんと おとうさんは しごとに おくれそうだった。
「ミミ、いそいで。がっこうに もっていく くだものを ひとつ
えらびなさい。」

On **Friday** Mum and Dad are late for work.
"Hurry Mimi, choose a piece of fruit to take to school."

わたしは　くだもので　いっぱいの　ボウルを　みた。
オレンジ、リンゴ、ナシ　どれに　しようかな？
リンゴと　ナシの　いろと　かたちは　まるで
おばあちゃんが　どようびに　つくる　スープの
なかに　はいっている　チョーチョーみたい。

I looked at the bowl full of fruit.

Should I choose an orange, an apple or a pear?

The apple and pear; their colour and shape remind me

of the cho-cho in Grandma's Saturday Soup.

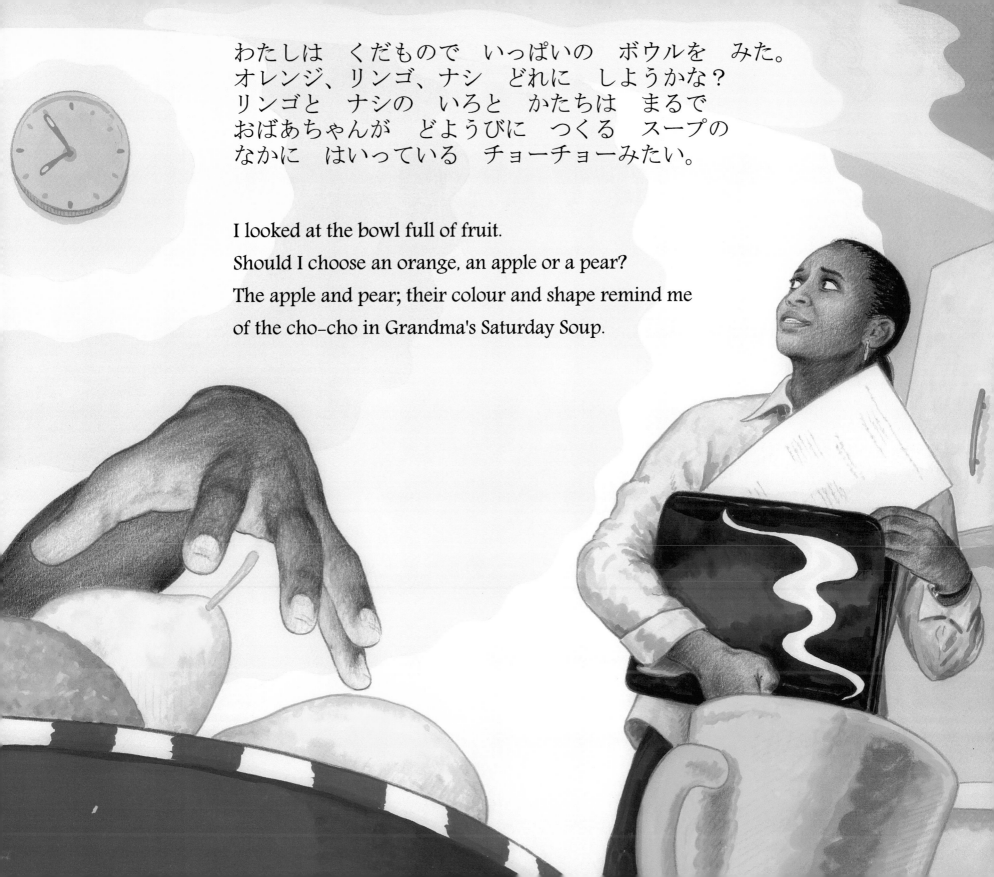

おばあちゃんは　ジャマイカの　くだものの　はなしを　してくれる。
「ジャマイカでは　がっこうに　いく　とちゅう、きに　なっている
くだものを　とるのよ。みずみずしくて　あまく　じゅくした
マンゴーをね。」

Grandma tells me about the fruits in Jamaica.

"In Jamaica you can walk to school and pick a piece of fruit

from a tree, a ripe mango all juicy and sweet."

がっこうの　あと　テストで　いいてんを　とった　ごほうびに
おかあさんと　おとうさんが　えいがに　つれていって　くれた。
おひさまが　でていたけれど　まだ　さむかった。
そろそろ　はるが　きたみたい。

After school, as a treat for good marks, Mum and Dad took me to the cinema.

When we got there the sun was shining, but it was still cold.

I think springtime is coming.

えいがは　たのしかった。いえに　かえるころには　ひが　しずみはじめていた。
しずんでいく　たいようは　おおきく　オレンジいろで　おばあちゃんが
どようびに　つくる　スープの　なかの　かぼちゃみたい。

The film was great and when we came out the sun was setting over the town.

As it set it was big and orange just like the pumpkin in Grandma's Saturday Soup.

おばあちゃんは　ジャマイカの　ひのでと　ゆうやけの　はなしを　してくれる。
「おひさまは　あさ　はやく　のぼり　とても　きもちが　よく　きょうも
がんばろうと　おもうの。」

Grandma tells me about the sunrise and sunsets in Jamaica.

"The sun rises early and makes you feel good and ready for your day."

「ひが　しずんで　つきが　でたら　なんまんと
いう　よぞらの　ほしが　きらきらと
ダイヤモンドの　ように　かがやくの。」
なんまんもの　ほし　なんて　そうぞうできない。

"When it sets and the moon comes out she is followed by a million stars
that look like diamonds twinkling in the night sky."
A million stars, I can't even imagine that many.

どようびの　あさ　ダンスの　おけいこに　いった。
おんがくは　ゆったりとした　さみしい　きょくだった。

Saturday morning I went to my dance class. The music was slow and sad.

おばあちゃんは　カリプソの　リズムや　スチールドラムを
こかげで　えんそうする　ひとびとの　はなしを　してくれた。
りっぱな　きの　はっぱは　むいた　グリーンバナナの
かわの　よう。
「おんがくを　きくと　たのしくなって　おどりたくなるのよ。」

*Grandma tells me about the rhythms of calypso music and steel drums,
of people playing under the shade of a tree. A wonderful tree with long
leaves that look like the strands of skin from a green banana.
"The music makes you happy and want to dance."*

おけいこが　おわって　おかあさんが　くるまで　むかえに　きてくれた。
みちを　くだって　がっこうの　まえを　とおりすぎた。
こうえんを　ひだりに　まがり、としょかんの　まえを　とおった。
まちを　とおりすぎて　えいがかんに　でた。そろそろだ。

Mum picked me up after class. We went by car.

We drove down the road and past my school. We turned left at the park and on past the

library. Through the town, there's the cinema and not much further now.

わたしは　おなかが　すいていた。とっても　ぺこぺこ。
やっと　おばあちゃんの　うちに　ついた。

I was hungry. Really hungry. At last we arrived at Grandma's.

げんかんに　むかって　はしっていくと
おいしそうな　においが　してきた。
グリーンバナナ、チョーチョー、ヤマイモ、
おだんご、じゃがいも、そして　カボチャ．．．

I ran to the front door and could smell a delicious smell.

It's green bananas, cho-cho and yams, dumplings, potato,

and pumpkin...

ねぎ、とりにく、おばあちゃん　とくせいの
ちょうみりょうに　とりがらで　つくった
たっぷりの　だし。
おばあちゃんの　サタデースープだ！

spring onions, chicken, a good pinch of Grandma's
country seasoning and a lot of chicken stock.
It's Grandma's Saturday Soup!

にちようび　ともだちを　よんで　うちで　しょくじを　した。
おかあさんと　おとうさんは　りょうりが　とても　じょうず。
でも　わたしが　せかいで　いちばん　すきな　たべものは
おばあちゃんの　つくる　サタデー　スープ。

On **Sunday** we had friends at our house for dinner.

Mum and Dad are good cooks, their food is nice but my favourite

food in the whole wide world is **Grandma's Saturday Soup**.